Siani

Shetland

Troll Carnival
The Old Surgery
Napier Street
Cardigan
SA43 1ED
www.trollcarnival.co.uk

First published in 2008
Published in 2004 as *Siani'r Shetland* (Gomer Press)
Translated by the author 2008

Text: ©Anwen Francis
Cover & interior illustrations: ©Pamela Cartwright
Glossary illustrations: ©Hayley Acreman

ISBN: 978-1-905762-620

Design: www.theundercard.co.uk
Typesetting: Lucy Llewellyn

British Library Cataloguing in Publication Data
A catalogue record of this book is available
from the British Library

Printed & Bound by Gomer, Llandysul, Wales

Siani

Shetland

Anwen Francis

TROLL
CARNIVAL
WWW.TROLLCARNIVAL.CO.UK

To my bundles of joy – Soffia and Henri.

Chapter 1

'Happy birthday to you, happy birthday to you,' shouted Rhys as he burst through the door waving a parcel in the air. He roughly snatched the duvet off her bed.

'Wake up will you, wake up,' he shouted as he grabbed her legs and pulled her down towards the bottom of the bed.

He'd already bought his sister a birthday present and knew she'd be delighted with it. He'd carefully chosen a wooden framed picture of a pony and he couldn't have chosen anything more to her liking.

'Oh be quiet, Rhys. It's half term – no school

today,' said Beca, throwing a pillow at her brother.

'You are nine years old today, Beca, and I have a present for you,' he said impatiently.

Beca sat up with a smile. 'Nine years old,' she said excitedly. 'I'm nine years old today!'

She jumped out of bed clutching her present and ran downstairs to the kitchen.

On the kitchen table sat a birthday cake decorated with green icing with a pink pony on top. A silver bell hung from the pony's neck. Her aunts and uncles, grans and grandpas had also sent gifts. But to her disappointment, there seemed to be just a card from her parents. On their many shopping trips to town, she had admired a little brown fluffy pony standing in the front of the toy shop window. Her mother knew that she would have liked it on her birthday. Never mind, thought Beca, she might have him for Christmas and then she could cuddle him in bed on the cold wintry nights.

Beca heard her mother come in and take off her wellies before entering the kitchen.

'It's cold out in those stables this morning,' said Mrs Lewis.

Both her parents worked hard on the farm and as well as helping her husband milk the cows at six o'clock in the morning, every morning, Mrs Lewis also mucked out the stables. They owned two hunters who had been idle since the foot and mouth epidemic and now Mr Lewis had decided to show them at local shows instead of hunting with them. Besides, he didn't have the time to exercise them every day and Beca was too young to ride them. Rhys was football and rugby mad and showed no interest in the horses or any other animal on the farm.

'Happy birthday Beca darling,' said her mum, planting a kiss on her daughter's cheek. 'Have you opened your card yet?'

Beca already knew that because of the foot and mouth epidemic, money was short and she could not expect an expensive present, but she had hoped, oh how she had hoped that she would have had that furry toy pony on her birthday. She also knew that the little pony wouldn't fit into the small envelope before her.

'Well open it, Beca. Don't look so miserable,' urged her mum. 'It's your birthday after all,' she added with a smile.

'Yes, come on,' said Rhys. 'You haven't opened my present either. Give it to me,' he said. 'I don't really think you want it.' And with that he grabbed the present and ran around the kitchen, waving it about in the air.

Beca ran after him, knocking over the kitchen stools in the chase. Rhys, being older and taller, held it too high for Beca to reach and seeing her eyes well up with tears said 'Say please, then.'

'Please, please, please,' she said with a sugary smile, hastily blinking away her tears.

She opened the parcel and was delighted when she saw that Rhys had bought her a super picture of a pony grazing in a meadow, awash with colourful buttercups and daisies.

'Oh thank you, football head,' she said. 'This will look fantastic on my bedroom wall. I really, really like it.' She wanted to give him a kiss and a hug but knew that Rhys wouldn't appreciate any soppiness.

And then, she opened the blue envelope. The kitchen was very quiet with all eyes on Beca. Rhys was in on the secret and could barely hide his excitement. There was a picture of donkeys on the front of the birthday card and Beca held it up for her brother to see.

'Look,' she laughed, 'A picture of you and your mates.'

'Ha, ha, ha. Now open the card,' said Rhys impatiently. 'Read the message.'

It said:

Happy Birthday Beca.

Hurry up and get dressed. We are going to Llanybydder horse sales to buy you a pony.

Lots of love and kisses

from Mum and Dad.

She stared at the card. Had she read it correctly? Did it really say what she thought it said? She could hardly speak.

'Are you really going to buy me a pony – a real live pony of my own?' she asked breathlessly.

Suddenly, the kitchen door opened and her father came in to join his family.

'Yes, Beca,' he said, grinning at his daughter. She hugged him tightly around his waist. He stank of cows but for once she didn't mind.

'Oh thank you, thank you,' she said. 'This is my best birthday ever. And thank you too Rhys, for your lovely picture.'

Rhys hated any silliness and began chasing her around the big kitchen table. She fled upstairs to prepare for the trip.

Chapter 2

Their journey in the lorry took them an hour and finally they arrived at the sales. They parked alongside other lorries, cars, vans and cattle trucks in the large parking ground. The town square was full of tradesmen selling farm tools, saddlers selling saddles, bridles and 'horsey' things, a woman with some cackling geese in a big cage and in the back of a car nearer the horse sale, a rough looking man had six terrier puppies for sale. The black and white puppies looked at Beca and usually she would have shown some interest in them and tried to touch them through their cage, but not today. She was thinking of the pony she was going to have and hoping that somewhere in the huge shed, the right pony was waiting for her.

'Stay close to me now Beca,' said her mother. 'Horse sales are dangerous places for adults and children alike.'

'Okay,' said Beca with a sigh. 'But hurry up mum, before all the horses are sold.'

As they entered the huge shed, they could hear the farmers, horse dealers and other people talking and laughing. They could see some leading and others pushing their horses and one woman shouting 'Watch your backs, stallion coming through.'

Above all this noise and commotion, they could hear horses neighing.

Suddenly, Mrs Lewis grabbed Beca towards her as a man rushed past them leading a very excited Welsh cob. She was a young filly, not accustomed to being in a sale with all its strange sounds and people everywhere. Her eyes were wide and wild, her nostrils flared with terror and she held her short tail up high. There seemed to be chaos and panic everywhere that Beca looked and she felt very small and frightened. She hid her face in her mother's coat. After the sound of the filly's hooves faded away, Mrs Lewis and Beca made their way further into the shed. Beca could see the auction rings and that's where the sales would begin at midday. She felt very nervous and excited.

There were over a hundred horses inside, some were small, some enormous, some were in foal and some were very, very thin and looked sad and bewildered.

'A few of the ponies look frightened,' said Beca sadly.

'Yes,' said her mum. 'Some of these horse sales can be very cruel places and sometimes you see things that are upsetting. But come on Beca, let's see if there's a suitable pony for you.'

'What about that one?' asked Beca, pointing her finger at a grey mare shivering in a dark corner of her pen.

'No,' said Mrs Lewis. 'She looks too frightened and nervous and not suitable for a child to ride her. Unfortunately, some of the ponies here today in the far end of the shed will be sold for meat. They will go to the continent where people eat horse meat.'

Beca shivered at the thought.

'Come along Beca, I can see some smaller ponies over there.'

They walked further along the crowded aisle, being jostled and pushed around by people who seemed to be in a terrible hurry to get somewhere.

'What you need is a Welsh mountain pony or something similar – a mare or gelding would be fine – a pony can be so much fun.'

Beca ran over to the gates.

'Oh mum, look at these ponies.'

There were seven ponies in one pen. Some were fairly wild, rolling their eyes and neighing loudly. Others seemed to be in a state of shock and looked around in bewilderment.

Beca looked at each one in turn, wishing that she could take them all home to Parc yr Ebol Farm. But she knew that she would have to choose just one and that it would means hours of brushing and mucking out – but also hours of fun and loving friendship.

'Look at that one over there,' said her mum, leading her over to a small, black mare.

'She comes from the Shetland Isles in Scotland.'

Although Beca had dreamed of having a brown or chestnut pony, she followed her mum politely to the pen. And there she set eyes on a furry black mare, standing strongly and squarely on four short furry legs. Her thick black tail reached to the floor and her eyes were hidden behind a long thick mane and forelock.

'Hello,' said a deep voice from the depths of the pen. 'Are you looking for a pony for this pretty young lady?'

The owner was big and burly and had a rather frightening booming voice but when he smiled his face smiled all over and his kind face was wreathed in wrinkles.

Although he towered above them all, he was gentle as he patted the little mare on her head and scratched behind her ears. The mare, in turn, nuzzled her soft nose against his rough tweed jacket.

'Yes,' replied Mrs Lewis, 'a pony who's kind and considerate but with a little sparkle as well. Something safe and dependable with a leg in each corner.'

'She's just the one for you then,' he said. 'Come inside the gate,' he added. 'You can stroke her, she's a real softie, but can be quite naughty sometimes like all little girls,' he said, looking at Beca with a twinkle in his eye.

With a nervous chuckle, Beca and Mrs Lewis entered the pen.

'You can stroke her. I have four children at home and she's used to having them around her,' said the owner, taking out a dandy brush from his pocket and tidying up the mare.

Beca bent forward and cautiously stroked the pony on her neck. The pony came closer and as Beca blew gently into her soft nostrils, she knew that she'd found a friend.

'Hello,' whispered Beca and the pony licked her hand with her warm, moist tongue.

'Well, they seem to like one another,' said the man.

'Yes,' said Mrs Lewis. 'How much are you asking for her?'

'Let me see, let me see,' he replied. 'She's very intelligent, used to loud noises on the farm, good at loading into the lorry and is not too naughty when the farrier calls to trim her hooves.'

'How old is she?' asked Mrs Lewis.

'She's seven,' replied the farmer.

'What's her name?' asked Beca.

'Well now, we call her Fluffball at home because she has such a thick coat, but her proper registered name is Morag Black Magic. She's registered with the Shetland Pony Stud Book Society in Scotland. We don't really have time for her and that's why we've decided to sell her. She loves company and needs a good home.'

Beca could think of several names for the pony – Black Beauty, Stargazer, Frolic, Fantasia – but not one of them really suited the pony who was watching her closely from under her thick forelock. Then suddenly, the pony grabbed hold of her scarf, and with a toss of her head, pulled it down to the straw on the floor of the pen.

'Oh you naughty shortie Siani,' exclaimed Beca with a laugh. 'That's it, I'll call you Siani – Siani Shetland.'

The pony neighed as if she agreed with Beca and rolled her eyes again as Beca scratched underneath her chin.

'Is she a quiet ride?' asked Mrs Lewis.

'Oh yes,' replied the farmer. 'When she was younger, I took her to a local show and she behaved very well. She took first prize for the best Shetland under three years old. She has a passport – and you must by law have passports for ponies these days. And if you don't want to ride her, you could always breed from her. Her father, or sire as they call them in the horse world, won first prize and champion at the Royal Show in England,' said the farmer with pride. 'So she's very good in all situations – used to tractors and the like on the farm and she's a good solid mare to ride and all of my four children rode her.'

Mrs Lewis decided to inspect the mare. She raised her tail, ran her hands down the mare's legs to feel for any lumps or bumps and checked her teeth.

'Does she have any vices or bad habits?'

'She doesn't kick or bite, she enjoys her food and you'll have to watch her weight, but other than that, she's perfect.'

Mrs Lewis looked expectantly at the farmer and raised her eyebrows.

'Well, how much?' she enquired.

'Let's see. You seem to be a good, caring family and it's important that the pony goes to responsible and kind people ... mmmm ... three hundred and fifty pounds, and not a penny less.'

'It's a deal,' said Mrs Lewis as she shook his hand and smiled. 'There you are Miss Beca Lewis – your birthday present, but on one condition, that you look after her well.'

'Oh yes, oh yes, I will, I will,' said Beca excitedly. 'And thank you mum, thank you, thank you.' She planted a wet kiss on her mum's cheek and grinned at the farmer before planting a kiss on Siani's muzzle.

'You have a fine new friend there, Beca. I can see that you'll make a good team. Now then, I'll come with you to your lorry,' said the farmer as he slid a blue head collar on to the pony.

'The head collar and the travelling rug are included in the price,' he added.

Together, they fastened the blue rug around the pony so that she wouldn't feel cold whilst travelling.

They picked their way cautiously back to the lorry in the car park, opened up the back door and Mrs Lewis led Siani up the ramp. But suddenly Siani was afraid and took two or three steps backwards. Beca spoke soothingly to her and bit by bit, she walked into the lorry. She looked around with her big, big eyes, she took a long drink from the water bucket and started eating the sweet hay from the hay-net tied to the wall of the lorry. Mrs Lewis tied Siani securely, closed the ramp and went to pay the farmer. 'Thank you,' he said and taking a £5 note from the wad of notes he gave it to Beca saying 'Five pounds for luck.' He touched his cap and returned to the sale.

'Happy then?' asked Mrs Lewis.

'Happy?' asked Beca. 'I'm the happiest girl in the whole wide world and this is my very best birthday. Thanks mum.'

Chapter 3

Rhys eagerly awaited their return. He'd been miserable since their departure that morning and had been idly shooting at targets with his toy pistol. Then they arrived and he 'shot' at the tyres of the lorry shouting 'bang, bang … bang, bang.' He was not a lover of horses or ponies and felt jealous that Beca had had such an expensive present for her birthday.

'Well Rhys,' said his mum as she went to lower the ramp of the lorry. 'Have you been helping your father this morning?'

'Yes,' he answered, too readily, and then added 'A little bit.'

Rhys could be quite lazy and helped his father as little as possible. His friends often came to play with him and farm work was the last thing on his mind. He wanted to be a footballer. He wouldn't mind being muddy on a football pitch but hated the mud on the farm. In fact, he hated living on a farm full stop!

Beca knew that her mum would have to resume her work on the farm before long, so she urged her to help her with Siani before she went.

'Come on, mum. Siani wants to see her new home,' she shouted.

The ramp was much too heavy for her to pull down but Mrs Lewis soon had the lorry open.

'Don't you dare make loud noises with that stupid toy gun of yours,' she warned her brother. 'Siani is very sensitive as all ponies are, and I don't want her frightened.'

Siani stood looking at them through her dark forelock. The hay-net was almost empty, but it was no surprise to Mrs Lewis who knew that Shetland ponies were very greedy little animals.

Rhys blew a loud raspberry and pointed his gun at the mare.

'What's that?' he questioned.

'That's my new Shetland pony and she's called Siani,' answered Beca.

'And put that gun away.'

'Siani, Siani – shorty Siani. What kind of name is that? And which way is it facing? It can't see where it's going. Look at the state of that mane. Call that a pony?'

He put his hands on his hips and laughed loudly.

'That's enough, Rhys,' said Mrs Lewis impatiently. 'She's a lovely little pony. Shetlands come from the Shetland Islands north of Scotland. It's so cold there that they need thick coats, manes and tails to protect them from the snow, wind and rain. Right Beca, you lead her down the ramp and into the small stable.'

Siani was quite sweaty after the journey and seemed reluctant to follow her new owner down the steep ramp.

'Don't you worry about a thing my little twinkle toes. There's a cosy stable ready for you. And then tomorrow, you can explore the field and meet some of the other horses,' said Beca. 'This is your new home and we'll be so happy together.'

Hesitantly, they walked down the ramp and

over towards the stable.

'Well, what a beautiful little Shetland,' said Mr Lewis with a smile. 'She's as black as a winter's night.'

'She's perfect, daddy, and so friendly. Siani is the best pony in the world,' said Beca and hugged her around her thick neck. 'Thank you.'

'Oh, I do like the name you've chosen. Bring her over here, so that I can take a closer look,' he said.

However, Siani had noticed some long grass growing on the other side of the yard and without any warning, she pulled hard on the lead rope and Beca had to let go. Away she cantered, across the yard with a few playful leaps and kicks, over to the grass.

They all laughed and Siani, with her mouth already full of juicy grass, looked round at them, wondering what all the fuss was about!

'You'll have to show her who's boss,' said Mrs Lewis. 'You never know what a pony will do next, so be prepared,' added her mum with a wink and a chuckle.

'She can't go into the show ring behaving like that,' said Mr Lewis. 'Right, let's take her into the stable.'

But as Beca approached, Siani had a different idea and kept bucking and cantering round the yard – only stopping now and then to grab tufts of grass.

'Mum, you'll have to help me,' said Beca, folding her arms. 'I just can't catch her. Naughty Siani,' she shouted across the yard.

'I'll catch her now,' said Mr Lewis. He went over to the feed shed and returning with a bucketful of pony nuts, he turned towards the stable, rattling the bucket as he went.

Siani pricked up her ears and in no time at all, she had crossed the yard and was obediently following Mr Lewis. But she was still thinking of all the long juicy grass that she'd left behind. She stood still for a moment, looking from left to right, from grass to bucket, rubbed her foreleg with her teeth, snorted loudly and trotted back to the grass.

'Siani, you come back over here this minute,' said an exasperated Beca, 'and stop messing about.'

'Come on, Siani,' said her father and gave the bucket a really good shake. To everyone's surprise, the greedy little Shetland followed Mr Lewis to the stable. He stepped inside, beckoning her with the bucket of pony nuts.

The stable was welcoming, with a deep bed of fresh straw, a bucket of water in one corner and a bulging hay-net hanging in the other. In she stepped and was rewarded with the pony nuts in the bucket.

'Good girl, Siani,' said Mr Lewis kindly. He slipped the head collar off the pony and watched her guzzle the nuts. He stepped outside, closed and bolted the half stable door and followed his family into the kitchen for lunch. It had been such an exciting morning.

Beca was so excited that she couldn't dream of eating her lunch. Her birthday had been so eventful that she could think of nothing else.

As the rest of the family tucked into their lunch, she imagined riding her new pony into the show ring and winning the first prize. She imagined being presented with a big red rosette and a huge silver cup. It had been her dream since seeing her father showing and winning with his horse years ago – and now she had the chance of doing the same thing.

'Beca, eat your lunch. It's cold out there today,' said her mum, refilling her mug from the teapot.

'Oh mum, I really can't eat. I'm so excited and I want to check if Siani's alright.'

'Well Beca, since it is your special day today, off you go. But be careful in the stable won't you. Siani needs time to get to know you and her new surroundings. It must be very strange for her,' said Mrs Lewis.

Siani had finished the pony nuts and when Beca peeped over the stable door, she was naughtily kicking the now empty water bucket around the stable.

'Hello Siani,' said Beca happily. 'Oh you are a beautiful, gorgeous pony and you're all mine.' She ran across the yard to get the tack box from the storehouse. It was overflowing with horse shampoo, brushes for manes and tails, coat and face, various coloured sponges for eyes, nose and bottom. There was also a hoof pick for cleaning the horse's hooves. Beca used this tool every time she caught a pony from the field to rid stones that get lodged in the foot. The stones have to be removed before they damage the soft inside of the hoof.

Chapter 4

Beca removed the travelling rug and started brushing Siani gently – the soft face brush for her face, a stiffer brush for her mane and tail and a dandy brush for her body and legs. Siani was thrilled with all the attention and stood fairly still for half an hour while Beca talked to her and brushed her until her coat shone like glass.

'Good girl,' said Beca and planted a big wet kiss on the pony's head.

'You have been busy, Beca,' said Mrs Lewis, 'and Siani looks so smart. You must be starving after all that hard work. Come on, your tea is on the table. I'll stay here and tidy up the stable and then I'll be in for a cuppa.'

After Mrs Lewis tidied up the straw bedding, washed and refilled the water bucket and topped up the hay-net, she took a syringe from her pocket and squeezed the contents into the side corner of Siani's mouth. Siani shook her head as she obviously didn't like the taste of the medicine.

'Sorry about that Siani,' said Mrs Lewis sympathetically. 'I don't suppose it was very nice but that medicine will get rid of all those nasty worms in your tummy.' She stroked underneath Siani's jaw and throat to ensure she'd swallowed it all, and then to Siani's delight, Mrs Lewis gave her a juicy carrot as a treat.

It had been a tiring and eventful day and soon Siani was fast asleep on her thick bed of straw.

Chapter 5

Beca awoke very early the following morning and smiled as she remembered the events of the previous day. Her bedroom walls were covered with posters of horses and famous riders – David Broome, the famous Welsh show jumper and a larger one of Ellen Whitaker, her heroine. On her bedroom chest of drawers was a framed photograph of her father's horses and on the floor by the window was an enormous stack of horsey magazines. Although she'd read them all from cover to cover, not one was thrown away in case she wanted to refer to something or other. She had not seen her bedroom wallpaper for a few years!

'Beca,' shouted her mum from the bottom of the stairs. 'Your breakfast is ready and Siani is neighing for hers too.'

Beca ran down to the warm kitchen in her pyjamas, gulped her orange juice, pulled on her wellies and before her mum could say 'hello,' she was half way to the stable to see her pony.

Mrs Lewis sighed and put the plate of bacon and eggs to keep in the warm Aga and followed her daughter to the stable.

'She looks fine, doesn't she,' said Mrs Lewis.

'Put the head collar on her and take her to see the other horses in the field. I'll come with you just in case we have a bit of trouble with those hunters. You'd better get changed first Beca – you can't go into the field in your jim-jams!'

'Wait for me, then, mum. I won't be a minute,' said Beca.

Mrs Lewis led Siani over to the big field and Beca carefully opened the gate. The mare seemed a little wary of the big field and the big horses, but when she saw the luscious grass, she got excited, then frightened as the hunters

galloped towards her from the top corner of the field. Mrs Lewis unfastened the head collar and suddenly, Siani bucked and cantered past the hunters without as much as a glance and raced to the top of the field. The hunters turned and cantered after her.

'Oh mum, will she be alright?' asked Beca in a panic.

'Don't worry. We'll watch from here and see what happens,' answered her mum.

Siani and the hunters galloped round and round the field, snorting as they went. Her short little legs were tired and she was eager to tuck into the abundance of grass surrounding her.

Suddenly, the brave little mare stood quite still and stared at the big horses thundering towards her. She looked terrified but determined. Beca held her mother's hand tightly.

'It's alright Beca. That's how horses behave when they first meet each other. Let's go back to the house. We'll check up on them when we've had some coffee and you've eaten your breakfast.' said her mum reassuringly.

Siani trembled as the two hunters approached and then with a shrill whinny, she side stepped them and galloped around the field with her tail in the air like an Arab horse would, with the two hunters in pursuit.

The three cantered round and round the big field, their tails held high, their nostrils flaring, their manes flowing wildly in the gentle breeze that blew in from the sea. Siani was tired and her little legs could go no further. She slowed down to a trot and then walked towards the gate, her coat glistening in the sun.

Although it looked as if the two big hunters were chasing her, all they really wanted to do was be friends. Suddenly the three began munching the grass and everything was quiet and peaceful once more.

Siani had never been in such a big field before. At her last home – near the mountains – her field was small with poor grass. But here, she felt she could get lost in the tall, rich pasture. She remembered the succulent clover leaves growing in the upper corner of the field. That would be her favourite place.

She made her way slowly up to the corner, keeping in line with the thick hedge. She peered through a gap in the hedge and saw that her new home was very near to the sea. Her very first home had been by the sea and she could remember being taken down to the beach for a hack when she was younger. They were wonderful days and now she was back in paradise.

Chapter 6

Siani spent two enjoyable days getting to know the field and the other horses. Every day, Beca would bring her a carrot or a juicy red apple from the orchard behind the farmhouse.

But soon, the half term holiday had ended and it was time for Rhys and Beca to return to school.

'Do I really have to go, mum?' asked Beca. 'I can't leave Siani here on her own.'

Her mum smiled.

Although Beca couldn't wait to tell her school friends about Siani, she didn't want to be parted from her either.

'You must go to school and try hard so that you have a well-paid job eventually to help pay for keeping Siani when you're older,' explained her mum.

'Yes of course,' she answered. 'See you later Siani,' shouted Beca through the open window of the car on her way to school. Siani glanced at the retreating car and then continued munching the dew-coated grass.

Siani had settled well in her new home and the two big field-mates were her friends. She spent her days sleeping and eating, occasionally rolling in the sand in the top corner of the field to get rid of her woolly winter coat. She'd been fortunate that she'd been bought by such a kind and caring family.

The big grandfather clock in the house chimed four o'clock. Siani heard something noisy coming up the lane and then saw the big yellow school bus stopping outside the farm entrance. School was over for the day and Rhys and Beca were home.

'Siani ... Siani ... Siaaaaaani Shetland,' shouted Beca, as she ran towards the field dropping her school bag in the middle of the yard.

'Oh Siani, I have missed you so much today. I've told all my friends about you and Elan, Rachel and Claire are dying to meet you,' said Beca spreading her hand through the mare's thick mane.

Rhys had fled to his bedroom to play on his Playstation 3. He had no time to mollycoddle any pony, let alone one his sister owned. Beca decided to take Siani for a short walk. She took the headcollar from the stable and as her parents were busy gathering the cows for the milking parlour, decided against asking them for help. She entered the field and caught Siani. She hadn't changed out of her school uniform which she always did before venturing out on the farm, but as she was only taking Siani for a short walk, she didn't bother.

She walked Siani to the stable and gave her coat a brisk brush to get rid of the dust, and then led her towards the farm lane which eventually joined the main road. Beca remembered Siani's previous owner saying that she didn't mind the sound of traffic. Since it was such a beautiful afternoon, Beca decided to show Siani the view of the beach and blue sea nearby, and in order to save time, ventured

34

across Mrs Hwmffra's farmyard next door. As it was milking time, the couple would go unnoticed. The view from the yard was breathtaking. Beca could see Cardigan Island and Poppit Sands in the distance, and a few yachts on the sea, their sails shimmering in the sunlight. Mrs Hwmffra had a donkey called Aneurin. Aneurin was a very special donkey as he had the longest ears in Wales. Beca hoped that one day, Siani and he would be good friends, but time was getting on and she decided to head for home.

Suddenly, a loud bang from one of the big sheds shattered the silence. Beca was startled but Siani was terrified. Her big eyes rolled in their sockets and she trembled all over. Gasping, Siani took a few backward steps and in a matter of seconds, reared, kicking her front legs wildly. Beca had no hope of holding her and the pony broke loose. There was another loud bang and Siani galloped blindly towards the farm entrance. Beca was numb with terror and turned just in time to see Siani disappearing around the corner, her black tail flowing wildly in the wind.

Beca ran after her and called her. She

realised that Siani was heading for the busy main road. But Siani didn't want to hear Beca. All she could think of was getting away from something that had terrified her. It was what every horse would do – it is in their nature to flee from danger.

The shed doors opened and there, repairing their rally car, were the two Hwmffra boys, Harry and Ifan, quite unaware that they'd had visitors and that now Siani was heading for the dangerous road with Beca in hot pursuit.

Luckily, Siani had calmed down and Beca eventually found her in Mrs Hwmffra's vegetable patch. Mrs Hwmffra was well known in horticultural circles and had won many prizes at local and national shows with her wonderful vegetables. Siani also thought they were wonderful and trotted excitedly through the lush growth. Then, seeing an apple tree in the corner, she munched first one, then two, then a third red apple from the tree. Beca knew that Mr and Mrs Hwmffra could be rather awkward and her parents often referred to them as 'the miserable people next door'. She crept quietly up to Siani and carefully made a grab for the lead rope, but Siani had seen her coming and was soon trotting through the vegetable patch again, pausing to snatch a huge carrot from the bucket by the garden gate – carrots meant for the family supper!

Mrs Hwmffra decided to fetch the bucket of carrots, opened the back door and was faced with Siani, cantering past carrying the juicy orange carrot in her mouth! Mrs Hwmffra was hysterical, waving her arms above her head and screeching.

'Beca Lewis, what's that black hairy creature done to my vegetable patch? Just you wait till I phone your mother!'

Chapter 7

Unfortunately, another neighbour of Beca's – Miss Tomos – had been driving along the main road when she had to brake suddenly to avoid colliding with the mare. Siani took no notice of her and, cantering happily, turned around in the middle of the road and overtook Miss Tomos, who saw her heading back for Parc yr Ebol Farm. Beca, who was still being shouted at by Mrs Hwmffra, was very relieved to see Siani turn into their farm entrance. Siani found a peaceful place behind the muck heap and then started munching the huge juicy carrot. Contentment was written all over her face!

Mrs Hwmffra and Beca arrived in the yard in Mrs Hwmffra's little red van. Beca looked upset but Mrs Hwmffra was furious. Her lips were shut tight and were blue, her chubby cheeks were scarlet and her dark eyes were open wide. She stepped out onto the yard in her yellow wellies and looked menacingly around the farm.

'Where are your parents?' she enquired sharply.

'Probably still milking,' whispered Beca. She was in a pitiful state, her cheeks stained with tears and perspiration. Mrs Hwmffra marched over to the milking parlour and without a word, barged into the cool shed. Beca found her contented pony basking in the sunshine, quite unaware of the mayhem she had caused.

'Oh Siani, what have you done? Mrs Hwmffra is furious and mum and dad will be so cross with the both of us,' whispered Beca into the pony's ear. She cuddled her pony and as she laid her head on the pony's neck, her tears flowed, leaving a damp patch on the thick black coat. Then she led her back to the stable.

A few minutes later, Beca heard Mrs Hwmffra leaving the farm revving her engine as she went.

'Beca, Beca where are you?' shouted her mother from the milking parlour.

'I'm in the stable,' answered Beca in a frightened, squeaky voice.

'What have you been up to, Beca?' asked her mum, giving her daughter a despairing look.

Beca didn't answer – she really didn't know what to say.

'Beca?' asked her mother again. 'Answer me.'

She tried to explain, but her mother was angry and impatient.

'Take the pony to the field, go to your room and stay there until I finish milking. Mrs Hwmffra is terribly upset. Do you realise that you and Siani could have caused terrible damage this afternoon? And someone could have been hurt very badly.'

Beca led Siani to the field, and then crept up to her bedroom where she threw herself onto her bed and sobbed. She cried herself to sleep and was woken by the chimes of the old grandfather clock striking six o'clock. Her parents were usually in the house by this time. She felt so miserable but decided that since she was now nine years old, she would not cry in front of her parents and certainly not in front of her brother. He'd been playing on his computer since arriving home and now decided to look for his sister. However, her bedroom door was locked. He rattled the door and gave it a few bangs with his fist.

'Go away, Rhys,' said Beca.

'What's the matter?' he asked.

'Just go away,' she replied.

'Be like that then,' he said and as he ran down the stairs, his parents were entering the kitchen.

'Beca's locked herself in her room and she won't talk to me,' muttered Rhys before his parents had had time to remove their working clothes.

They had already talked about what had happened and they were wondering whether Siani was too headstrong a pony for their daughter. They didn't want Beca, or Siani or anybody else to be hurt and they had already decided to sell the pony.

Mrs Lewis went up the stairs to Beca's bedroom and knocked on the door. Beca unlocked it and let her mother in. She realised she could not hide away for ever.

Beca couldn't believe what her mother was

telling her – that Siani was too strong, too wild and too headstrong and that Beca herself was too young and irresponsible to handle the mare and that they had decided to sell her!

'No, I don't want you to sell her, she's my very best friend!' shrieked Beca and with a wild swipe of her hand, scattered the books off the top shelf of her bookshelf.

'Don't be silly, Beca,' scolded her mum. 'We'll talk about this later when you behave like a nine year old.'

Mrs Lewis returned to the kitchen to prepare supper for the family and left Beca cursing and stomping around her bedroom.

Suppertime was unusually quiet. Even Rhys, who usually drowned everyone with his football talk, was quiet. But Beca was far from quiet. Her stomping and kicking and screeching and thumping echoed through the farmhouse. She had never gone without her supper before and had never been in such a pitiful state.

The phone rang just as Mrs Lewis was putting Beca's supper in the oven to keep warm. She heard Rhys saying:

'Beca? She's in her bedroom and won't come down for supper,' he told the caller.

Mr and Mrs Lewis glanced at each other and Mrs Lewis took the phone from Rhys. It was one of their neighbours – Miss Tomos who had very nearly collided with Siani that afternoon.

Miss Tomos had always been fond of horses and had won many championships with her own. She also gave riding lessons on her farm or would travel around the area giving lessons to various children and pony clubs. She had been very worried about the black Shetland she'd seen and after asking several people about her, had been told that she belonged to Beca, Parc yr Ebol. She wondered if she could pop around to see her.

'I'm sorry Miss Tomos, but we've decided to sell her as she's not suitable for Beca,' said Mrs Lewis.

'Oh please don't sell her,' pleaded Miss Tomos. 'Let me come and see the two of them together and if I don't think they're suitable, I'll be willing to find a good home for her. But if I'm satisfied that they suit each other, perhaps I can give them a lesson every week. What do you think about that, Mrs Lewis?' asked Miss Tomos.

'Thank you for your offer. You're very kind.

I'll have a chat with my husband and I'll phone you later on this evening,' said Mrs Lewis.

Rhys listened to his parents discussing Beca and Siani. He was just a little bit fond of the pony but was jealous of the attention given to Beca. He hated being in the background but was unable to do anything about it.

Mr and Mrs Lewis decided to give Siani another chance – with the help of Miss Tomos.

Huh thought Rhys. *I would like a new football kit too, and a trip to see Manchester United play, but there is never enough money for that. It isn't fair.*

Beca was overjoyed when her mum told her about keeping Siani and Miss Tomos's offer of lessons. She hugged her mum, ran downstairs to eat her supper and then hurried over to the field to give Siani a special hug.

Rhys could see the two through the kitchen window. He felt jealous of the pony. Beca and he used to play together before the pony arrived on the farm. Now, his sister had no time for him. He crept upstairs and lay down on his bed, gazing moodily at the ceiling of his bedroom.

Miss Tomos was coming early next day and the evening was turning wet and windy. Beca brought Siani into the stable. She gave her a thorough brushing until her coat shone. She then gave Siani some fresh hay and water. Beca hummed happily to herself as she bolted the half stable door and skipped across the yard towards the welcoming warmth of the kitchen.

Rhys got up to draw the curtains and saw Beca coming towards the house. She was looking so happy now that her little pony was to have another chance. Slowly, he smirked. He had an idea that would get rid of that horrid pony for ever.

Chapter 8

Miss Tomos arrived early next morning and toot tooted her way into the yard. She was always early, never late, especially when the meeting was anything to do with horses. Siani looked out over her stable door. She'd slept really well on the thick bed of straw and although she had plenty of hay in her hay-net, she wanted to return to her field with its luscious grass and sweet patch of clover. She also missed her two friends.

'Hello little pony,' said Miss Tomos cheerfully as she strode towards the stable. Siani neighed loudly. She enjoyed attention.

Beca and her mum walked towards the stable and saw that Miss Tomos was already inside talking soothingly to Siani and stroking her thick fluffy ears. Beca was ever so pleased when Miss Tomos said: 'Well, isn't she a quiet pony. She has very good bone and is in tip top condition. Look at that shiny coat.'

Rhys watched from the kitchen doorway as Miss Tomos asked Beca to lead Siani around the yard. All went well and then she asked Beca to run so that Siani would trot beside her. Siani obeyed and then they returned to the stable. Miss Tomos and Mrs Lewis watched as Beca tied the mare to a piece of baler twine tied to a ring on the stable wall and brushed her mane and tail. Siani enjoyed every minute.

'Would you like to ride her today, Beca?' asked Miss Tomos.

'Oh yes please, Miss Tomos,' said Beca, hoping her mother would approve.

With a smile and a wink, Mrs Lewis went to get the saddle and bridle from the tack room. Beca ran to put on her special riding hat, her gloves with grippy palm pimples and her long riding boots.

Mrs Lewis put the saddle firmly but gently

on Siani's back and fitted the bridle over her head. Mrs Lewis gave Beca a leg-up onto the pony's back and after settling down, the two walked around the yard. Miss Tomos thought that they looked very comfortable together and as she watched the two, she asked Mrs Lewis lots of questions about Siani. She wanted to know everything about her and asked to see the field and the other two horses.

Rhys was very angry at the way things were going. And overcome with sheer jealousy, he decided to act. He ran over to the shed to get his football. Mrs Lewis and Miss Tomos were busy taking about the other horses by the field gate and Beca and Siani were walking away from him. This was his chance! Suddenly, he kicked his football and it hit Siani squarely on her bottom. Fortunately for him, the ball rolled behind some tyres. Siani had a terrible fright and with a leap in the air, cantered out of the yard, past the two ladies nattering away with Beca struggling to stay on her back. But Beca was not balanced in the saddle and didn't have the experience to know what to do. Although she held onto the mane with both hands, she flew off and landed on the hard ground.

Mrs Lewis and Miss Tomos ran towards her. Her nose was bleeding and she'd had a dreadful fright. She got up shakily. Her jacket and trousers were muddy and torn but, luckily, the hard hat saved her from serious injury. Siani had disappeared!

Chapter 9

'Siani, Siani, come back!' sobbed Beca, wiping her nose on her sleeve.

'I told you that Siani was wild,' said Mrs Lewis to Miss Tomos.

'Something must have startled her,' explained Miss Tomos calmly. 'A pony wouldn't just bolt like that, especially one with such a calm disposition.'

But Rhys was the only one who knew the truth and he was beginning to feel guilty. Everything had happened so quickly. He hadn't meant for his sister to fall off and hurt herself. His idea of frightening both Beca and her pony was starting to go horribly wrong.

'It wasn't Siani's fault,' agreed Beca, drying her eyes. 'Something did startle her.' She glanced around the yard looking for clues and wondered if Rhys had played a part in it. He had been behaving oddly since Siani arrived, maybe he was jealous, thought Beca.

'Now then,' said Miss Tomos firmly. 'Our first priority is finding that pony before she is injured or before she hurts someone else. A frightened pony is a dangerous one.'

Mrs Lewis told her husband what had happened and added that she was going to look for Siani with Miss Tomos and Beca in the van.

Rhys watched the van leaving the yard, saw his father go the bottom field and decided to keep quiet about the accident. Beca, again, was the centre of attraction and he did feel angry and jealous. He knew that if someone found out what he had done then there would be a big row and he'd probably lose his football for ever! He crept across the yard and over to the stack of old tyres. He reached for the hidden ball, ran to the barn and hid it under a huge pile of straw. He knew that he should not have thrown the ball at the pony and he was now worried that something awful was going to happen down the lane. He ran back to the house, upstairs and into his bedroom.

Siani was nowhere to be found. They looked for her all day, asking everyone if they'd seen her. They looked in fields and gardens, behind sheds and garages, but with no luck. Siani was well and truly lost. Soon it was milking time again and Mrs Lewis had to return to the farm.

'Please, mum, don't go back. What if someone has stolen her? Someone might sell her in the meat market for the continent,' pleaded Beca, and she began sobbing again.

'I'm afraid the cows have to be milked and I don't suppose Rhys will think of helping. He is very moody these days,' said Mrs Lewis.

'You go back with your mother and I'll go on looking for Siani. I'm sure she's around here somewhere,' said Miss Tomos kindly.

'I'm coming with you, Miss Tomos. I can't sit around thinking and worrying. I must help find Siani,' said Beca.

'It might be best if you come home, Beca. Miss Tomos will contact us as soon as she has any news,' explained her mum.

Beca felt angry. She huffed and puffed and began to plead.

'Mum please, please, please. I must find Siani and bring her home,'

After listening to her daughter beg and beg, Mrs Lewis finally decided to give in.

'Alright, but you must be back home by midnight. Good luck.'

The family spent a miserable night at the farm. Rhys felt guilty that he was responsible for the worry he'd caused, and all because of his stupid jealousy. He couldn't sleep and kept imagining the most dreadful things. Mr and Mrs Lewis spent their time phoning around the farms in the area just in case someone, somewhere had spotted the little black pony, who must be very frightened now that it was getting dark.

Chapter 10

Beca arrived home at midnight. They'd had no joy and Siani was nowhere to be seen.

'We shall start our search in the morning, Beca. Try and sleep now so that you can be bright and alert tomorrow. I'll pick you up at eight o'clock sharp,' said Miss Tomos.

'Thanks, I can't bear the thought of Siani all alone and lost in the dark,' sobbed Beca.

'Think positive thoughts, Beca Lewis,' said Miss Tomos and gave Beca a wink as she drove off home.

Mrs Lewis greeted Beca at the door with a mug of hot chocolate – her favourite.

'Both dad and I have left the stable door open hoping that during the night Siani might return,' said her mum. 'Now go to bed and try and get some rest. You'll need your energy for the morning.'

At six o'clock the following morning, Beca bounced out of bed as she heard the milk lorry coming down the driveway. She ran out of the farmhouse, across the yard and over to the stable. Maybe Siani had returned during the night. But when Beca looked inside, the stable was still empty, the water and hay untouched. Cari the sheepdog usually greeted her with furious barking outside the kitchen door but she didn't seem to be about the farm either. She always welcomed the milk lorry with loud yapping and woke up the whole family at the same time, but not today.

Beca didn't want her breakfast. She was so worried about Siani, and Cari too.

'I'm sure you'll bring Siani back later on,' said Mrs Lewis, trying to comfort her daughter. But she was worried about the black mare and secretly wondered if she had been stolen.

'No, we won't. She's gone forever!' shouted Beca, and started crying yet again. 'I'm sure she's been stolen, and where is Cari – she must be hungry. She hasn't eaten last night's supper or today's breakfast,' she wailed.

Mr Lewis ate his breakfast quietly and then went to herd his flock of sheep into the yard. He had to check their feet often to see if they were alright. They made such a noise that Mr Lewis didn't hear Miss Tomos arriving.

She parked her car in the entrance to the farm and had to wave her arms in the air to catch Mr Lewis's attention.

'I've got some news for you,' she shouted above the bleating of the sheep.

'Good news I hope,' he said.

Beca saw Miss Tomos's car and ran out to greet her.

Miss Tomos beamed. 'Come with me, Beca, bring your mum and dad too. We won't be long. Quickly now, forget about the sheep, Mr Lewis,' she ordered.

In the car she told the family how she'd found the pony and Cari the sheepdog. She'd been searching all night and was overjoyed to have found them safe and well.

'Oh Miss Tomos, you're the best!' screamed Beca in a fit of laughter.

'Well done, Miss Tomos,' said Mr Lewis. 'Are we heading for the beach?' he asked.

'Yes, that's where they are. Siani has grazed her nose but is alright and Cari is looking after her,' she answered.

Beca could see two black dots at the far end of the long beach. As they grew closer, she recognised the pair. They were both wet and Siani hung her head miserably. But Cari, on seeing her master, ran to Mr Lewis, her tail

wagging furiously. Beca put the head collar on Siani and kissed her face all over. The pony was very quiet. She trembled and looked very sorry for herself.

'I wonder how Cari found her,' said Miss Tomos.

'She could probably see her through the hedge. She loves sitting there watching the seagulls and sometimes, if she's feeling naughty, she'll bark and run after them,' answered Mr Lewis.

'It was the barking that drew my attention to them,' said Miss Tomos. 'She's a very clever little dog and she must love Siani very much.'

'I'll lead Siani back to the farm,' said Beca.

'And I'll walk with you,' said Mrs Lewis, giving Siani a big hug.

'Alright,' said Miss Tomos. 'I'll take Cari and Mr Lewis in the car. See you in half an hour.'

'Oh Siani, Siani,' squealed Beca. 'I thought I'd never see you again.'

'Careful Beca. She's had a frightening experience,' said Mrs Lewis as they made their way back to Parc yr Ebol Farm.

They had quite a way to travel to get home. They had to walk the length of Patch beach near Cardigan Island, over to the slipway where the boats were launched, then onto the main road. The farm was at least a mile and a half from there, and they had to walk up Trwyn yr Allt hill which isn't for the faint hearted. Beca, Mrs Lewis and Siani were all exhausted as they turned into the farm entrance.

Beca led Siani to the stable and after eating some sweetly scented hay and drinking nearly a bucketful of cool water, the pony slumped down on the thick bed of straw and slept. Cari was given extra food to eat and she was so exhausted that she slumped onto her doggy bed and slept by the welcoming warmth of the Aga.

Supper time at Parc yr Ebol that evening was a happy affair until Mr Lewis said that Siani was too wild for Beca to control. Unfortunately for Beca, her mother agreed.

'Please don't say that she has to be sold, I can't bear it!' pleaded Beca, her eyes brimming over with tears.

The three began arguing and shouting, her father bringing his fist down hard onto the table with a loud bang.

'She'll have to...' he said, but before he could finish his sentence, Rhys came in.

'It's all my fault,' he whispered sheepishly.

All eyes turned towards him.

'What did you say?' asked Mrs Lewis.

'It was my fault. I threw my football at her to frighten her.'

'Oh, you nasty, horrible boy,' hissed Beca.

'Hush, Beca,' ordered Mrs Lewis. 'Why, Rhys? Just tell us why you would do such a wicked thing.'

'Because since Siani came here, nobody has time for me. It's all Beca and Siani, from morning till night,' he explained sadly.

'That's not true, Rhys. Your dad and I love the two of you equally. What you did was stupid and dangerous. Beca and Siani could have been badly hurt,' she said, raising her voice slightly.

'I'm really sorry, I'm really, really sorry,' said Rhys, trying hard not to cry in front of his family.

Suddenly, Beca jumped up excitedly and smiled.

'Does this mean I can keep Siani after all?'

Chapter 11

Summertime was always a busy time at Parc yr Ebol. Mr and Mrs Lewis had been gathering the hay and Rhys had been helping too. Beca and Siani had weekly riding lessons with Miss Tomos and had even started jumping. Lessons were expensive and since Mr and Mrs Lewis could not afford to pay Miss Tomos, she was only too pleased to accept straw bedding for her own horses instead. Beca and Siani had learned so much from the lessons and by now, Beca was in charge and Siani enjoyed doing what her mistress asked her to.

It had been another hot day and as the

family had been working hard, they went to bed quite early – grateful for the coolness of their bedrooms. The old grandfather clock struck nine o'clock as they walked past it towards the stairs.

And as Mr Lewis turned the kitchen lights off, his mobile phone rang. Who could that be, he thought as he fumbled in his trouser pocket for his phone.

'How are you boyo?' said Mr Lewis as he made his way from the kitchen to the hall. 'What? Call the vet, and I'll be with you now,' he shouted. 'Anna, I must go. That was Dai. His prize winning cow is having trouble calving. I'll be back later,' he shouted to his wife. 'Don't wait up for me,' he added as he grabbed his coat and ran out to the Land Rover.

Beca and Rhys were usually allowed to watch the television until nine o'clock on Friday and Saturdays, but tonight, no one complained when told to go to bed. It had been so hot, the evening was still warm and the horses had long stopped grazing and hung their heads down low in the field. Even Cari the sheepdog was fast asleep on the cool kitchen floor, twitching and flicking her tail as she dreamt her doggy dreams.

As the household slept in the quiet of the night, three strangers were travelling along the farm lane. Their white van turned into the farm entrance. One of the men opened the gate quietly and, with no headlights, the van drove slowly into the yard. The three men walked around the farm, snooping here and there, nearly invisible in their dark clothes. One man fetched a heavy stick from the boot of the van and walked with the others to the front door of the farmhouse. Poor Mrs Lewis had been so tired that evening that she'd forgotten to lock the door and with a wink and a nudge, the three men tiptoed into the hall. They moved about so quietly that even the normally alert Cari remained asleep.

But Siani had seen them from the field. She had seen them arrive, watched them as they looked around and was waiting to see if they would enter the house. She didn't have long to wait either. The door opened and she watched the three men carrying something long and heavy out into the yard. It was the valuable grandfather clock which had belonged to Mr Lewis's great grandfather! The clock chimed a quarter to twelve. Siani started neighing as loud as she could and kicked the gate with her sturdy legs. With her broad, flat teeth she tried to undo the thick rope which held the gate so that she could get out and alert the family.

'Shut that 'orse up,' hissed one of the men to the others. 'It's going to wake up the neighbourhood.'

'How?' asked the dimmest of the three.

'Like this you bird brain,' he replied and threw a heavy stone at Siani.

Luckily, the stone narrowly missed her ear but Siani had realised that these men were dangerous and she had to wake the family. She neighed and neighed and kicked her hooves against the gate.

'What's the matter with Siani tonight?' thought Beca from her bed. She went to the window and peered into the darkness.

'Oh my goodness,' she shouted and ran to her parents' room.

'Mum, mum, phone the police, we've got burglars!'

Mrs Lewis immediately phoned 999, her face pale and her hands trembling so much that she could hardly hold the receiver. If only her husband was home! Beca ran into her brother's bedroom to wake him.

'Sssshhh,' she whispered. 'We have thieves in the house!'

Both children made their way into their parents' bedroom and carefully peered from the window.

From behind the curtain, the family watched the three men struggling to get the big, long clock into the back of the van. They were careful not to be noticed in case the men returned to the house and attacked them.

'Rhys, phone dad on his mobile. Tell him what's happening,' said Mrs Lewis. 'If only your dad was here now, he'd have his gun at the ready!' she whispered.

Within minutes, a siren could be heard approaching the farm. The police car was on its way and now she could see the flashing blue light bobbing up and down on the other side of the hedge.

The burglars had heard the siren too and, panicking, they argued and swore at each other, pulling and tugging the clock, one pushing and shoving it and the third one swearing and shouting at the other two. There was no time to lose and he ran to the front of the van to start the engine for a quick getaway.

'Come on, you two, the cops are heading this way!' he shouted. 'And I don't want to get caught!'

Cari woke up with a start and, hearing strange voices, she started to growl. Something wasn't right and she decided to investigate. Through the glass kitchen door she could see shadows – shadows of three people. She smelt the air, and knew that these men were trouble. She barked fiercely, growled and howled. She had to alert the family.

In the large field near the farm entrance, Siani had managed, with her teeth, to undo the rope that tied the gate, and now she stood firmly by the entrance, her nostrils flaring, her eyes flashing in the moonlight and her furry legs stomping rhythmically. No one was going to get past her and escape down the lane.

'Siani,' shouted Mrs Lewis from her bedroom window. 'Siani, get out of the way. They'll run you over!'

The van lurched forward and sped towards the entrance. Siani stood her ground, her tail swishing wildly. But nothing or no one was going to stop the panic-stricken thieves from making a getaway. With a sickening thud, the van hit Siani on her side and she fell motionless onto the road. She ached all over and blood spurted from her injured head onto the cold earth.

Chapter 12

When the burglars arrived at the end of the lane they could go no further – the police had parked their car across the lane to stop their escape.

'And where are you lot off to this time of night, eh?' asked one policeman.

'Oh, mmm, we had lost our way, Inspector,' answered the driver of the van, trying to sound as innocent as he could.

'You won't mind if we have a quick look in the back of the van then will you?' he asked, walking calmly to the rear of the van. The other two policemen stood close to the van in case the burglars tried to run away into the night. Cari also stood guard, growling and baring her sharp teeth menacingly at the strangers.

With that, Mr Lewis and the vet arrived in the Land Rover and headed towards the group of men and the police.

Mrs Lewis ran across the yard to her husband.

'They've stolen the family...'

But before Mrs Lewis could finish her sentence, the old grandfather clock in the van struck twelve o'clock. The mellow chimes echoed across the still of the night. There was no doubt that they were the burglars who had taken the valuable clock.

'What time is it Sarg?' asked one policeman with a wide smile on his face.

'Time for some straight talking Huw, I think,' laughed the Sarg and added 'Right boys, out of the van, hands in the air, nice and quiet now, no funny business.'

With towels for Siani's cuts and grazes, Beca rushed out through the door and straight over to her beloved pony, who was still lying on the floor. Beca could see her eyes rolling, hear her laboured breathing and see the pool of blood. Tears rolled down Beca's cheeks as she realised that Siani was very badly injured. Rhys was also upset.

'Poor Siani,' he said. 'Poor Siani.'

Luckily, Jeremy the vet was on the scene. He knelt down beside the little pony and examined every part of her still body.

'Well,' he said. 'This brave little pony is in a state of shock, but her legs seem fine. She has a bad cut on her forehead and has lost quite a bit of blood. Let's get her back to the stable. Keep her in for a week and I'll come to check her every day.'

Mr Lewis and Jeremy helped Siani to her feet and unsteadily made their way to the stable. Siani lay down with a long sigh and with the help of an injection was soon fast asleep. Beca knelt down on the warm straw, stroking Siani's cheek.

'You'll be alright, Siani,' she whispered. 'You'll be alright.'

Siani took no notice.

'She will be alright, won't she?' Beca asked the vet.

'I'm sure she'll be fine once the shock has worn off. Give her plenty of hay and fresh water. You can take her for a short walk once or twice a day when she's happy to be on her feet. Leave it a few days to see how she is. There's no point rushing things. Phone me if she's no better by the morning, but I'll be here around midday tomorrow anyway to check her,' replied Jeremy with a kind smile.

Chapter 13

The following morning saw several newspaper reporters, broadcasters and cameramen walking the yard. They'd heard the news of the burglary and wanted to know more. They wanted to speak to Beca, take pictures of the grandfather clock and, more than anything, they wanted to see Siani, the heroine.

Beca and Rhys ran downstairs and Beca hurried over to the stable to see how Siani was. Beca peered over the door and Siani was lying on her side and still fast asleep.

'Siani? Siani, how are you today?' asked Beca.

Hearing Beca's voice, Siani opened her eyes and took a draught of water from the bucket that Beca was holding in front of her. She ate a carrot and a handful of hay, then lay her head down again on the straw.

'Are you Beca Lewis?' asked the reporter of the local paper, peering over the stable door. 'Siani is your little pony isn't she? Is she better today?'

'Well,' answered Beca. 'She has eaten a carrot this morning so she must be feeling better.'

Another reporter asked 'What's so special about the mare then?'

'Siani is the best pony in the world and she's my very best friend,' answered Beca with a smile, hugging Siani around her thick neck. 'And she's also the bravest,' she added. 'She caught the burglars!'

Mr Lewis had just herded the cows back to the field after milking and joined Beca in the yard.

'If Siani had not neighed as loud as she did last night, the burglars would have got away with the grandfather clock – our family treasure would have been lost forever,' explained Mr Lewis. 'She's a very special pony and Parc yr Ebol will be her home for ever.'

Siani was famous. Her photograph appeared in all of the local and national papers, the story could be heard on radio stations across the country, and both Beca and Siani appeared on the television news. She was famous all over Wales. She was the most famous pony ever!

The three burglars appeared in court and they admitted that they had tried to steal the clock and had knocked the pony to the floor in an attempt to flee the farm. Mr Lewis told the story and the three were found guilty of attempted theft and cruelty to an animal.

Chapter 14

Jeremy the vet called twice daily at Parc yr Ebol Farm that week. Siani was given medicine in her feed bucket and the dressing on her forehead had to be changed every morning. Beca was pleased that Siani was slowly improving. There were a number of shows coming up and Beca was hoping they could go. But Siani had to be really better before then.

On the tenth day after the burglary, Beca called in on Siani on her way to school as usual. All her school friends had been to see Siani. Some had sent 'get well' cards and Beca had pinned them around the frame of the stable door. Everyone was surprised when the cantankerous Mrs Hwmffra called to see the mare with a bucketful of her precious carrots and apples. And Miss Tomos called three times a day to see her, bringing her sugar cubes as a treat.

That morning, Siani was on her feet and peering out over the stable door.

'Oh Siani, you're on your feet,' squealed Beca. This was very good news.

'Fantastic,' said Mrs Lewis with a smile. 'Leave her in the stable for today again and I'll take her for a short walk after lunch.'

Rhys was eating his breakfast when Beca ran in with the news and although everyone had forgiven him for kicking his football at Siani and causing such misery, he still felt a little guilty. He'd recently come to like Siani and had even spent some of his pocket money on a huge sack of carrots for her as a get well gift. He decided to call on Siani on his way to school. He threw his bag over his shoulder and carried his football under his arm. He liked to play with his school friends during breaks. He secretly pretended to be Ryan Giggs and aspired to be a famous footballer when he left school!

He walked into the farmyard and once Siani saw the football, she became nervous and fidgety. She was afraid that Rhys was going to kick the ball at her again! Rhys saw how agitated she was and knew that he shouldn't have taken the ball anywhere near her stable.

'It's alright Siani,' he said kindly. 'Come here, I won't hurt you.'

Siani walked nervously towards him, keeping her eyes on the football. She stopped. She was still afraid and started shaking and snorting.

'Okay then, I'll put the ball on the straw,' said Rhys.

He lay the football neatly on the straw beside Siani's hooves.

Within seconds, Siani lurched at the ball, then stamped on it with all her might. It burst with an almighty bang. She picked up the tattered ball and with her teeth, threw it out over the stable door, just missing Rhys's head!

Rhys was speechless. And then, he started laughing and laughing until he ached all over. He knew quite well that if Siani could talk she would have told him off for frightening her and that he was never to hurt her again. They understood each other at last and became firm friends.

The children on the school bus laughed themselves silly when Rhys told them what had happened.

'Oh, she is naughty!' laughed Beca and then she remembered that the blacksmith was calling to trim her hooves. 'I just hope she behaves herself when he's there.'

Siani had to have her hooves trimmed quite short so that she could walk comfortably. In a show, she would have to walk perfectly straight. Shetland ponies don't need to be shod unless they are used for pulling carts or are being ridden on the roads.

Elis, the blacksmith, arrived on time. Mrs Lewis had already cleaned Siani's hooves with a hoof pick ready for the trimming.

'Morning Mrs Lewis,' said Elis, looking over the stable door at Siani. 'She's a smart little pony, Mrs Lewis. She has a very pretty head.'

'Yes. She's quite special. We bought her for Beca on her birthday some months ago. We're very pleased with her even though we had a rocky start,' said Mrs Lewis with a smile.

'And famous too from what I heard on the

radio,' said the young blacksmith as he opened the stable door and walked in. He ruffled Siani's mane to settle her and Siani stood quite calm, her eyes closed in ecstasy.

'I'll stay with you, Elis. You might need some help,' said Mrs Lewis, putting a head collar on the pony.

'Oh, I don't think there'll be much of a problem with this little darling, but you are more than welcome to stay and watch,' said Elis. 'Now then, which leg should I do first?' turning his back towards the mare and kneeling down.

But Siani wasn't keen on having her hooves trimmed. Mrs Lewis noticed Siani open her eyes wide and stare at Elis. She thought that Siani looked naughty and she was right, because suddenly, she bit the blacksmith's bottom!

'Aw, wwww, aw,' shouted Elis, leaping into the air. 'Aw, she's bitten my bum.'

Mrs Lewis doubled up with laughter then wondered if Elis had really been hurt. He might need a doctor, or even worse – have to go to hospital. But Elis rubbed his bottom, laughed and said: 'A naughty little darling, Mrs

Lewis. Quite a character!'

His jeans were ripped, his underpants were torn and red teeth marks could be seen on his bottom! But his minor injuries didn't deter him from carrying on with his work.

'Now then Miss Siani,' he said, and ran his hand down her leg to pick up her hoof.

Siani looked very pleased with herself and neighed loudly just as if she was laughing with them. She decided to behave herself and allow Elis to get on with his work. Mrs Lewis held the lead rope tight and whispered in her ear, just as Beca would do.

'Oh you're a naughty one alright, but a loveable one!'

She took out a big, juicy carrot from her pocket and Siani crunched it noisily as Elis carefully trimmed the remaining three hooves, glancing now and again at Siani's head just in case she should fancy another bite of his behind!

Chapter 15

It was a beautiful day – the sun shone warm and bright and a gentle breeze blew in from the beach nearby. Just the weather for preparing Siani for the show the following day. Beca was up and about early and started by giving Siani a thorough brushing. Then came the shampooing. Siani didn't really like the shampooing or the rinsing with the cold water from the hosepipe, but she enjoyed watching the bubbles dancing rainbow coloured in the warm sunshine.

Beca brushed the mane and tail to untangle them and then with the help of her mother, she carefully plaited the long coarse hair so that in the morning, after removing the plaits, the mane and tail would be lovely and wavy. It took a long time and soon it was lunchtime. Beca put a rug onto Siani's back to keep her clean and warm and led her into the stable. Mrs Lewis prepared buckets of feed for all the horses while Beca brushed Siani's hooves and cleaned her eyes, her nose and her bottom with her different sponges. The judge would be looking everywhere for a speck of dirt!

'Is your shirt clean for the show, Beca?' asked her mum, later that evening.

'What?' asked Beca, not really listening to her mum.

'You can wear your school tie. Nobody will notice,' shouted Mrs Lewis from the feed room.

'Muuum! Everyone will be looking so smart and I'll be wearing my yucky school tie,' said Beca downheartedly.

She didn't want to be different to all the other competitors.

'Just the once, Beca,' said her mum. 'Then you can save some pocket money to buy a proper one for the next show.'

Mrs Lewis would have liked to have bought Beca a new shirt, tie, jacket, jodhpurs and riding boots, but money was tight. All horsey things were expensive and Beca would soon outgrow them.

'Beca, answer my mobile will you please. I've left it on the window ledge outside the stable. I'll be there now,' said Mrs Lewis.

'Mum, mum, it was Miss Tomos on the phone and guess what – she's managed to find me some second-hand riding clothes to wear tomorrow. Isn't that fantastic?' she said, jumping up and down excitedly. She hugged her mother around her waist and said: 'Siani and I will be the smartest pair in the show. And we're going to win a prize too,' she added, her face beaming as bright as the midday sun. Siani neighed loudly from the stable. Beca and Mrs Lewis laughed as they made their way wearily back to the farmhouse.

As they entered, the old grandfather clock struck nine o'clock.

'Now then, Beca, time for bed. You have a big day ahead of you tomorrow,' said Mrs Lewis, stifling a yawn.

'Goodnight Siani!' shouted Beca before

closing the door. But Siani was already fast asleep (quite unaware that she was going to a show the following day) dreaming of what ponies dream about. She sighed and twitched in her magical land of dreams.